PLAID BEAR
and the Rude Rabbit Gang

by P.K.ROCHE

THE DIAL PRESS • NEW YORK

HOME
SWEET
HOME

Published by The Dial Press
1 Dag Hammarskjold Plaza
New York, New York 10017

Library of Congress Cataloging in Publication Data
Roche, P. K. [Patricia K.]
Plaid bear and the rude rabbit gang.
Summary: While on vacation Plaid Bear and his three
friends encounter the rude rabbit gang.
[1. Bears—Fiction. 2. Rabbits—Fiction.
3. Animals—Fiction. 4. Gangs—Fiction] I. Title.
PZ7.R585Pl [E] 81-68774 AACR2
ISBN 0-8037-6986-5 ISBN 0-8037-6990-3 (lib. bdg.)

The art for each picture consists of an ink and wash drawing
with three color overlays, all reproduced as halftone.

Early one morning Plaid Bear left his comfortable home in Woodly to spend a restful vacation at Dingle-by-the-Sea. His best friends Sarah Mouse, Rod Panda, and Amanda Chicken went with him. They were almost there when some rabbits on bicycles came speeding by and bumped them off the road.

"I hope they're not going where we are going," said Plaid Bear.

Soon the four friends arrived in Dingle-by-the-Sea and stopped at a sidewalk café. As they were sipping cool drinks some rabbits came along and knocked Plaid Bear's lemonade into his lap. Then the rabbits hopped onto their bicycles and rode off.

"It's them again!" cried Rod Panda. "The rude rabbits!"

That night the four friends stayed in a hotel near the café. After dinner, at the hotel owner's request, Plaid Bear played his bagpipe for all the guests and made many new friends.

None of the new friends were rabbits on bicycles.

The next day the four friends went to the amusement park. Amanda Chicken carried her new sun umbrella. While they were riding the merry-go-round, some rabbits who were passing by made it whiz. Then they ran off, laughing and whooping. Plaid Bear recognized the rude rabbits even without their bicycles.

A small hound dog leaped onto the merry-go-round. He was too late to catch the rabbits, but he slowed the merry-go-round to a gentle stop. Finn Doggo was his name and he was Dingle-by-the-Sea's Chief of Police.

As Plaid Bear began to thank him they heard shouts and screams from far down the boardwalk. "Save my balloons!" "Oh, my jelly beans!"

With Finn Doggo blowing his whistle all the way, they rushed toward the hubbub.

Plaid Bear ran bravely into the midst of a mob of jelly-bean-hurling rabbits, but they tossed him in the air as if he were another jelly bean.

"You are a disgrace to the good name of rabbit!" yelled Amanda Chicken. Pretending not to hear, the rabbits turned up their noses and swaggered off.

Finn Doggo, who had stopped to question the balloon seller, was a little too late to catch the rabbits.

When Plaid Bear asked where the rest of the police were, Finn Doggo hung his head.

"I am all there is," he said. "And those rabbits are more than one hound can handle."

"You need help," said Sarah Mouse. And that was how Plaid Bear and his friends became deputy police.

With Finn Doggo they hunted the rabbits all over town, questioning everyone. But the rude rabbits had disappeared.

Plaid Bear and his friends took the next day off and went to the beach.
They put down their blanket and picnic lunch not far from where some
campers had pitched a tent. Then everyone hurried to take a swim.

It was a perfect day for the beach in Dingle-by-the-Sea. Sunny and warm,
with no chance of rabbits.

Unfortunately the campers were the rude rabbits! They had stayed hidden in their tent, peeking out until Plaid Bear and his friends were far into the water. Then the rabbits came leaping and tumbling out of the tent. They fell upon the lunch and gobbled up every crumb.

When the swimmers came out of the water, they found no lunch and many rabbit tracks in the sand.

"So that's who the campers are," muttered Plaid Bear. He tried to play his bagpipe for comfort, but it had sand in it and sounded odd. It could only wheeze and whooze. But this gave Plaid Bear an idea.

Late that night something large and long came slithering onto the dark, quiet beach. The thing stopped at the rabbits' tent. It breathed ever so softly. *Wheeze. Whooze.*

"Huh? Whuzzat?" grumbled a sleepy rabbit voice. A rabbit head popped out of the tent, and then another and another.

"Holy hopping hares!" gasped the boss rabbit. "It's a sea monster and it's coming for us!"

The rabbits were terrified until...

one of them noticed that the back of the sea monster had chicken's feet! He crept over and lifted an edge of the costume.

"Well, toast my tail!" roared the boss rabbit. "It's that loudmouthed chicken with the plaid marshmallow and their little pals! What do you mean by waking us up in the middle of the night in that silly getup?" Slowly the rabbits crept back. Some of them snickered.

"What's going on here?" called a voice near the tent. It was Finn Doggo, just in the nick of time! Quickly he arrested the rabbits and took them to jail.

"Those rabbits don't look so tough in their pajamas, do they?" remarked Plaid Bear.

The next day the rude rabbits stood before the judge in Dingle-by-the-Sea's courthouse. The judge told them they'd have to pay for the lost balloons and jelly beans, and he made them apologize to Plaid Bear.

"And finally," the judge said, "on Saturday next…

you must give a picnic for the whole town of Dingle-by-the-Sea!"

"But I'm a rabbit, not some twerp picnic-giver!" snapped the boss. The judge leaned down very close to answer the boss rabbit. "It's your choice," he growled. "You may spend next Saturday at your picnic—or in jail!"

Sure enough, the rabbits gave a splendid picnic.

Soon after the picnic the rabbits left town. It was also time for Plaid Bear and his friends to leave and go home to Woodly. They knew they would miss their friend Finn Doggo, but he promised to visit them.

"You'll find good food, good times, and good friends in Woodly," said Plaid Bear.

"And not even one rude rabbit!" added Amanda Chicken.

So they said their good-byes and set out for home.

After they had been traveling for a while—far in the distance—Plaid Bear and his friends saw some bicycle riders on the road ahead. They had long ears.

But they were no trouble at all.

Born and raised in Brooklyn, New York, P. K. Roche earned a B.A. from St. John's University and an M.A. from New York University. She learned to draw while studying with Caldecott Medal-winner Uri Shulevitz at his advanced workshop in Greenwich Village.

She has lived in Upper New York State and Cambridge, Massachusetts, and worked in a variety of areas: for a university agricultural research project, with an engineering firm, and as a copywriter for a classical music station, but she says that "no job has been as satisfying and as much fun—or such hard work—as writing and illustrating books for children."

She is the author of *Dollhouse Magic: How to Make and Find Simple Dollhouse Furniture,* and the author-illustrator of two books about a pair of mouse brothers: *Good-bye, Arnold!* and *Webster and Arnold and the Giant Box,* a Dial Easy-to-Read.

P. K. Roche now lives in Brooklyn with her husband, Jack, who is a lawyer, and their two children.